Christmas Gecko

Doris Noland

All Scripture references are from *The Message* or *New International Version* unless otherwise indicated

For Information: Hope Productions
Creations@joenoland.com

Printed in the United States of America

ISBN Paperback: 978-0-9755505-7-1
ISBN eBook: 978-0-9755505-8-8

Cover and Interior Design: Creative Publishing Book Design

Sweet Waioli

In the valley of Manoa
Lies the Sweet Waioli garden,
Sweet Waioli 'Singing Waters'
Next to Heaven, near my heart.

If you listen, you will hear it
Angels Singing in the garden
Sweet Waioli 'Singing Waters'
Songs of Heaven to my heart.

*Songs of blessing and forgiveness,
Songs of healing making whole,
Coming from the 'living waters'
So refreshing to my soul.

If you listen you will hear it,
Angels singing in the garden,
Sweet Waioli 'Singing Waters'
Songs of heaven, to my heart.

(Words and music by Doris Noland)

Red ginger Alpinia purpurata

Note: "Waioli" is translated "Singing Waters" from Hawaiian. All plant photographs in this book are taken from The Salvation Army's Waioli Gardens, located in the Manoa Valley, Honolulu, Hawaii, and represent the actual gecko habitat depicted in the story. They are but a sampling of the plants growing in this lush, tropical paradise. The cross pictured above (framed by the Red ginger) is located at the entrance of the historic Waioli Chapel.

Once upon a time in Hawaii's Manoa Valley there lived a little green gecko. He lived in the eaves of a big white house right next door to the Waioli Tea Garden.

*T*here were many geckos living in the lush, green gardens and they loved the shiny green leaves and moist, dark soil of Manoa Valley. They were happy in the beautiful gardens and didn't mind the daily rains. They sang and chirped night and day, enjoying a veritable banquet of insects that lived in the valley.

Coconut Palm

This particular little green gecko, however, didn't chirp. He didn't like the rain and refused to join the rest of the geckos when they called out to him: "Come and play. It's December and there's plenty to eat!" Silently, he ignored them and hid under the eaves of the big white house.

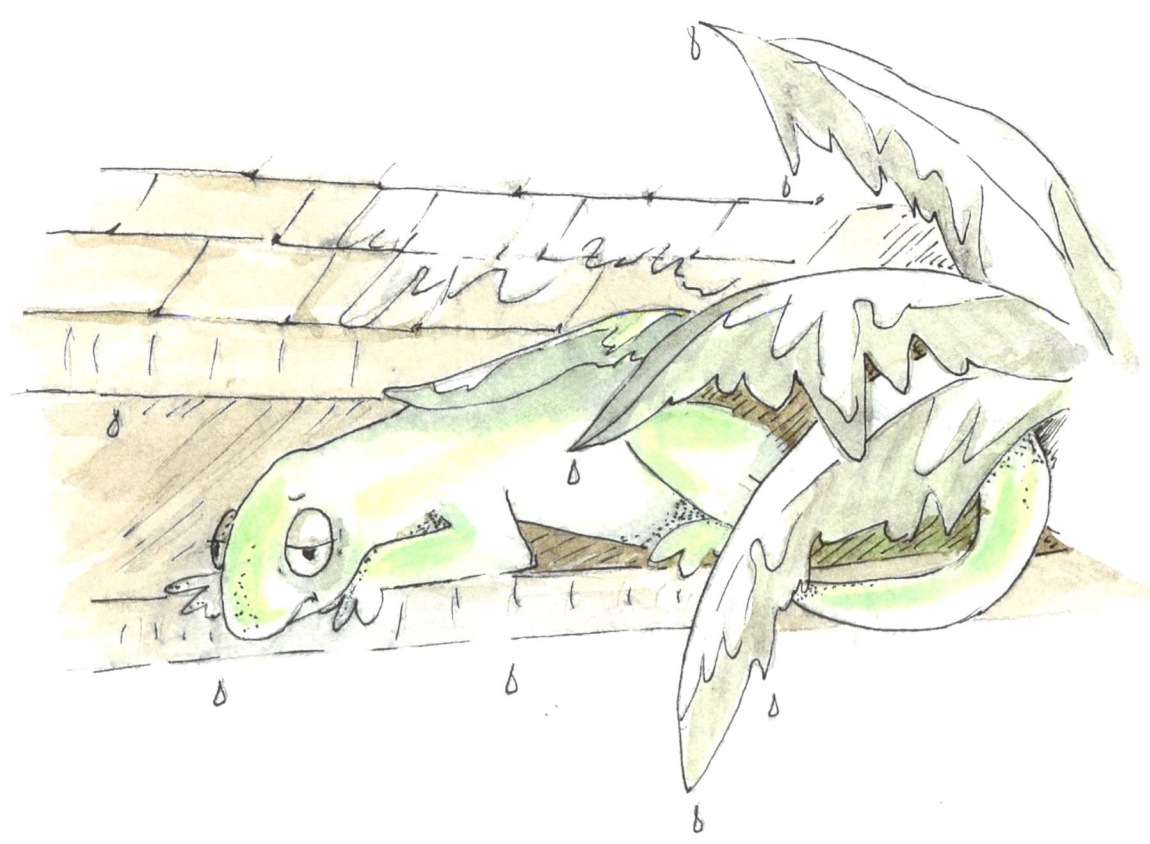

He grumbled and complained night and day, refusing to help the rest of the geckos control the hordes of mosquitos that hummed in the moist air. "We all must do our part to control the mosquitos in Manoa," said the Great Green Gecko.

But the little green gecko just sulked and complained, rain or shine, refusing to help and refusing to chirp like the rest of the geckos in the garden.

Monstera deliciosa Liebm

*T*hen one day in December, a most unusual thing occurred. The people who lived in the big white house came home with a large green tree tied to the roof of their car. *That is most unusual*, thought the little green gecko, moving closer to get a good look.

The man took the tree down from the roof of the car and carried it to the door of the house. *This is most unusual*, thought the gecko. He ran down the wall and jumped into the branches, as the tree passed through the door. *I must see what they are going to do with the tree*, he thought to himself, silently hiding among the pine needles. The smell of the tree was "most unusual," and not at all like the sweet fragrances so familiar in the Manoa Valley.

Wandering Jew

Quickly, the tree was set up in the corner window. *This is great!* he thought. *I can bask in the sunlight, and when it rains, I will be warm and dry.*

*J*ust as he was getting comfortable, the lady who lived in the house began tying pieces of colored ribbon and shiny glass balls onto the branches of the tree.

Zebra plant: Calathea zebrina

*T*he little green gecko was frightened and ran to the top of the tree, only to find a lighted star blinking off and on, off and on!

"**T**his is most unusual," he said to himself. "What can all this mean?"

Heliconia Lobster claw

When the lady seemed satisfied that every branch was properly decorated, she brought out a little brown box.

From inside the box, she took out a tiny shelter and set it under the tree. Next came the manger, a cow, two sheep, and a donkey. *Not much bigger than me*, thought the gecko. Two figures were placed in the shelter, one that looked like the woman and one that looked like the man. Three shiny figures were set out next. *As brightly colored as a chameleon*, thought the gecko. Last from the box came two children, one with a tiny lamb in his arms.

Ti leaf: Cordyline fruticosa

"**I** wonder what all of this means," chirped the little green gecko, "This is most unusual!" And he settled back into the tree.

All of a sudden, there was a "most unusual" noise and lights began to twinkle all around him. "Joy to the World," a music box chimed as it sat on the branches above his head.

Day after day, the gecko sat in the "unusual" tree. Every night when the man and lady came home, they would turn on the tree's lights and listen to the music box play, "Joy to the World."

Each night, the little green gecko would creep down to the tiny figures under the tree and be filled with wonder. *Most unusual*, he would think to himself, as he climbed back into the branches.

Plumeria

Then one night he noticed a very special excitement within the house. Visitors were arriving.

A little boy and girl danced around the tree. They clapped their hands when the lights came on, and sang with clear sweet voices, along with the music box as it played, "Joy to the World!"

At last, the children sat down beside the tree and the lady took out the little brown box. From inside the box, she took the last little figure and placed it in the manger. It was a tiny baby.

Most unusual, thought the little gecko as he edged closer to the little stall. *What can this mean?* he wondered.

Ohai Alii

*T*hen the man took a large black book into his lap, opened the pages, and began to read.

He read about a woman named Mary, and a man named Joseph, who went to a city called Bethlehem. There was no place for them to spend the night, so they stayed in an animal shelter on the edge of town. Mary had a baby that night and laid him in a manger because there was no crib.

Angels told shepherds that the baby was born. "Joy to the World," they sang (The little green gecko recognized that song!). Kings came with gifts for the baby, and they worshipped him. *What a wonderful story!* he thought.

Silently the little gecko listened as the man told how this baby was Jesus, the Son of God, who loved people of the world so much that He was willing to die to save them. "He sees every sparrow that falls," the big black book said. "Why, if He can see a sparrow, he can see me too!" chirped the little gecko, and his heart was strangely warmed.

Pagoda-flower

*T*hat night as the house lay sleeping, he climbed down the tree and crept up to the stall. Gazing down upon the infant, he remembered all that he had heard. *How selfish and lazy I've been*, he thought. *How I wish I could tell everyone this beautiful story, but what can a gecko do?*

*H*e looked into the face of the infant Jesus, then over to the shepherds with their sheep and the brightly attired wise men with their shining gifts. *I too would like to give the infant King something!* he thought, noticing that the baby lay exposed to the night air.

Dracaena family

"**I** bet there were mosquitoes there too. Why, if I'd been in Bethlehem, I would have eaten the mosquitoes humming in the manger. It would have been my job!" he chirped with some importance.

The more he thought about it, the happier it made him feel. "I'd do it just because I wanted to!" he decided.

About that time the little green gecko looked out the window into the Waioli Tea Gardens. A most unusual sight awaited his eyes.

There was a manger scene out in the garden, only much, much larger. Real animals and real people stood bathed in light and wonderful music filled the night air.

Watching, he noticed that the shepherds were scratching their necks and the wise men slapped their arms, while the mother Mary was trying very hard to keep the mosquitoes away from the manger.

People who had come to see the live nativity scene batted and slapped the air around them, finally turning away and going home, unable to enjoy the beautiful pageantry.

"This is awful!" cried the little gecko. "Everyone needs to hear this wonderful story!" He ran down the tree and squeezed through a crack in the window.

Monkey Pod

Running from branch to branch and leaf to leaf, he chirped out in a loud gecko voice, "Come on everybody. It's Christmas Eve and we have a job to do!"

"What's come over you?" cried all of the other geckos. "We're tired, we've worked hard all day long."

"Now, now!" the little green gecko chirped telling them what he had seen. "It's a wonderful story and the world needs to hear it," he implored.

"If it's made such a change in you, it must be wonderful indeed!" replied the Great Green Gecko. "Let's help!" they all cried out together, "For it's Christmas Eve!"

They chirped and sang as they scurried to the light. SNAP! POP! ZING! flashed their tongues as they darted from leaf to leaf.

Banana: Musa x paradisiaca mai'i

"**J**oy to the World" the music rang, and the little green gecko chirped and sang.

The shepherds stopped scratching and the kings stopped slapping themselves.

Mary smiled as the little green gecko climbed up on the edge of the manger fiercely attacking every mosquito that flew near the infant.

Bird of paradise: Strelzia reginae

Crowds began to gather, and people carried candles and stood listening to the Christmas Story.

When at last the music swelled, "Joy to the World," the crowd sang. The little gecko could hardly contain himself. "Joy to the World," he chirped, "Joy to the World!"

Areca Palm

That night when all was quiet the little green gecko slipped back into the house. He crept under the Christmas tree and smelled the fragrant pine.

"This has been a most unusual night," he said to himself and he fell asleep beneath the manger.

True aloe: Aloe barbadensis

In the morning the children came into the room and squealed with delight. "A Christmas Gecko!" they cried and lay on their tummies to get a good look. Sure enough, there he was quietly watching over the Baby Jesus.

Dracaena family

"**N**o mosquitoes will harm this baby," they said, turning on the tree lights. "Joy to the World," the music box played. "Joy to the World," the children sang. "Joy to the World," the little green gecko chirped happily.

Heliconia: Parrot's beak

Every year since that eventful night in the Waioli Tea Gardens, on the seven days before Christmas when the Living Nativity is shown, if you listen very carefully, there will be a most unusual sound heard in the leaves. It is the sound of a little green gecko happily singing...

"JOY TO THE WORLD,
   the Lord has come!"

THE END

Mango: Mangifera indica L

The Inspiration

In the early 1990s, my husband and I lived in the Manoa Valley in a home next door to the Waioli Tea Gardens where the world-renowned Waioli Tea Room resides. Every year the Salvation Army holds a Live Nativity Scene in this beautiful garden, and I could hear the music and see the Christmas scene from our living room window.

Geckos are aplenty in this area of the valley and often visited our home, hiding behind the pictures on the wall and resting on the top of our mantle clock. So, it wasn't too much of a surprise when after Christmas I discovered that a little green gecko had taken up residence in our Christmas tree. I had to virtually shake him out of the tree before I could pack it up for the New Year! Thus, came the inspiration for this little book... Christmas Gecko.

The Waioli Tea Gardens has a wonderful history in Honolulu. Operated by the Salvation Army, the campus was for many years a home for abandoned children. The Tea Room was a training place where the children learned skills in food service, cooking, baking, and sales. The historic chapel on the property was their place of worship. When the program was moved to a new location, the Tea Room remained as a lovely historical restaurant and a gathering place for the community. Visitors come from far and wide to be married in this historic chapel. Every year on Christmas Eve the traditional Christmas candlelight service is observed.

The message of Christmas as seen through the eyes of the little green gecko is a reminder that no matter how small and insignificant we may feel, there is always a way to serve God by using the gifts He has given to us.

"… It's a Wonderful story, and the world needs to hear it!" the little green gecko implored. "…Joy to the World – the Lord has come!"

DORIS

The papaya plant: Carica papaya

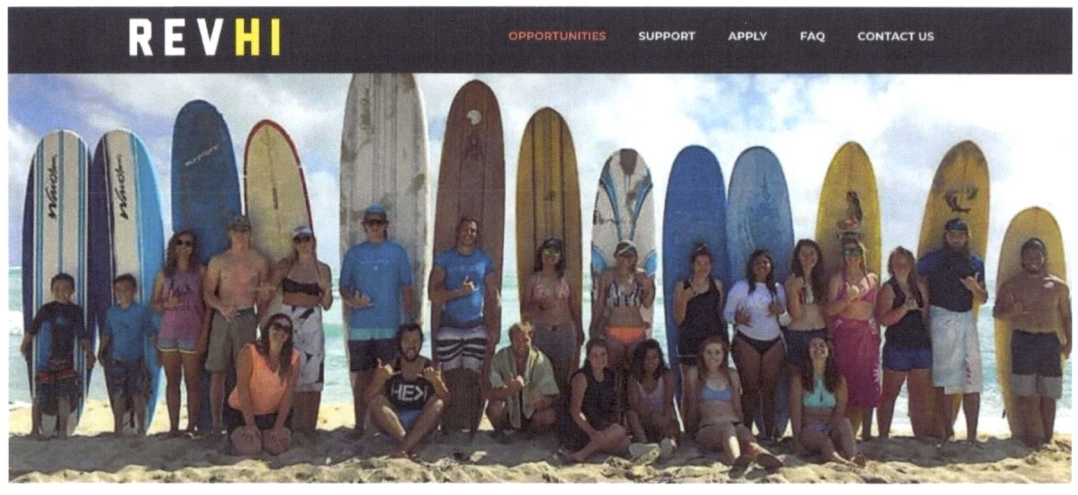

Revolution Hawaii is a mission intensive program for young adults between the ages of 19-29. It's byline: *A YEAR TO CHANGE A LIFETIME!* It was birthed in the Waioli Gardens, geckos galore inhabiting their dorms and keeping the mosquitos away. The mission of this program and the message of this book are compatible.

All proceeds from the sale of this book will go to financially support Revolution Hawaii. Donations are also solicited to help team members with scholarship assistance. For more information:

www.bit.ly/rev-hawaii
www.revolutionhawaii.com
www.themorerevolution.com/stories

When in Honolulu, Hawaii, visiting the historic Salvation Army Waioli Gardens and Tea Room is an absolute must!

To learn more about ordering this book
and other creative resources:

creations@joenoland.com
www.bit.ly/JN-books
www.themorerevolution.com

www.ingramcontent.com/pod-product-compliance
Lightning Source LLC
Chambersburg PA
CBHW042320250626

47164CB00016B/64